For my friend, agent, and idol Marcia Wernick,
who always knows just what to ask for
E. C. K.

For Staci, who didn't even ask for Osbert, but loves him anyway
H. B. L.

First edition 2004

Library of Congress Cataloging-in-Publication Data
Kimmel, Elizabeth Cody.
My penguin Osbert / Elizabeth Cody Kimmel ;
illustrated by H. B. Lewis. —1st ed.
p. cm.
Summary: When a boy finally gets exactly what he wants
from Santa, he learns that owning a real penguin
may not have been a good idea after all.
ISBN 978-0-7636-1699-1
[1. Penguins—Fiction. 2. Gifts—Fiction. 3. Christmas—Fiction.]
I. Lewis, H. B., ill. II. Title.
PZ7.K56475My 2004
[E]—dc21   2003040981

8 10 9

Printed in China

This book was typeset in Colwell.
The illustrations were done in watercolor, pastel, and digital rendering.

Candlewick Press
2067 Massachusetts Avenue
Cambridge, Massachusetts 02140

visit us at www.candlewick.com

My Penguin
Osbert

Elizabeth Cody Kimmel

illustrated by
H. B. Lewis

CANDLEWICK PRESS
CAMBRIDGE, MASSACHUSETTS

This year, I was very specific
in my letter to Santa Claus.

We've had a few misunderstandings in the past.
For instance, last year I asked for a fire-engine-red
racecar with a detachable roof, a lightning bolt
on the side, and retracting headlights.
And he did get me one.

But it was only three inches long.

And the year before, I had really wanted a trampoline. I wasn't sure how to spell it, so in my letter, I just sort of described what I wanted.

Santa sent me a pogo stick.

So this year, I was really, really careful. I wrote Santa a long letter and told him that I would like to have my own pet penguin. Not a stuffed penguin, but a real one, from Antarctica.

I told him my penguin should be one foot tall, white and black with a yellow beak, and his name should be Osbert. I included a drawing.

I put extra postage on the envelope and sent it off a whole month early.

Then I waited.

When Christmas morning came, I was the first one downstairs.

There he was!

He was black and white with a yellow beak, and exactly twelve inches tall. He was moving
and breathing
and everything.

Around his neck was a tag. It said:

Santa had come through!

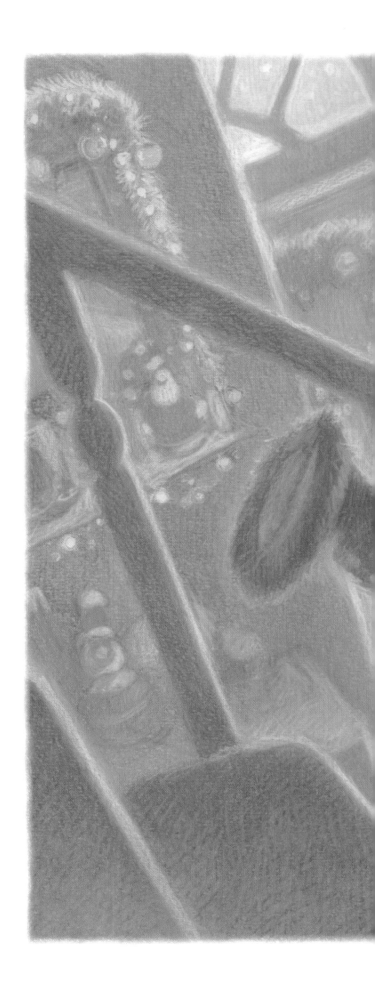

I wanted Osbert to meet everybody.
I wanted to take him to my room.
Plus, I wanted to open my other presents.

But Osbert really wanted to go outside
and play.

It was pretty cold, and kind of windy
too. There was a foot or two of snow
on the ground, and no sun.

But I had asked for Osbert,
and now I had him.

So we went outside.

We played powder slide and wreck-the-igloo.

We had snowball fights and made ice penguins.

We escaped from the jaws of imaginary leopard seals.

Osbert wanted to go swimming, but I explained
that it might not be possible. So we sang some
of the old penguin songs instead.

That night I was ready to go straight to bed. We'd had such a big day. But Osbert wanted to take a bath.

He filled the tub to the very top, and we got in. Osbert unwrapped all the bars of soap and floated them around like icebergs.

After a while, I had prune fingers, and my skin itched from all the soap.

But I had asked for Osbert, and now I had him.

And Osbert liked playing in a cold bath.

The next morning, Mom said she'd make ANYTHING I wanted for breakfast.

When I closed my eyes, I saw a stack of chocolate chip waffles with heated syrup, a platter piled high with fried sausages, and an icy pitcher of freshly squeezed mango juice.

But Osbert doesn't like rich food, and he doesn't like hot food, and he doesn't like sweet food.

Osbert wanted cold creamed herring with seaweed jam for breakfast.

So that's what we had.

After breakfast, it was my turn to do chores. So I did the dishes and went upstairs to clean my room.

When I came back down, I saw that Osbert had been working too. He had built an entire ice village out of freezer pops, frozen leftovers, and tubs of ice cream.

It was all beginning to melt.

Osbert, of course, couldn't hold a towel in his flippers.

But I had asked for Osbert, and now I had him.

So I cleaned up the mess myself.

That afternoon, when Osbert was watching
the weather channel on cable TV,
I secretly wrote Santa another letter:

Dear Santa,

How are you and Mrs. Claus? We are fine.

Thank you for the great penguin named Osbert.
We take cold baths together and have
creamed herring for breakfast.

I am getting used to spending all day
in the snow.

Plus, it turns out I didn't have frostbite after all.

your friend,
Joe

P.S. One more thing, Santa. If you feel like maybe
I should have asked for a different present,
and you want to swap, that would be OK.

And while Osbert was leafing through
a snow-globe catalog, I snuck out and
mailed the letter.

A couple of days later, I woke up to find a package at the foot of my bed. There was a tag with my name on it, signed

Santa

Inside the box was a red pullover sweater and two free passes to the grand opening of Antarctic World at the zoo.

After Osbert made a shrimp sculpture out of the wrapping paper, he wanted to go right away. But he didn't want to take the bus. The zoo was a long way away, but I had asked for Osbert, and now I had him.

So we walked.

When we got to Antarctic World, Osbert headed straight for the Penguin Palace.

There was a huge snowy hill with an ice slide leading down to a big pool. There were leopard seals painted on the walls. Tiny bergs of real ice were floating in the water.

And then a door opened in the wall, and a guy came out and started tossing creamed herring to all the penguins.

When it got to be closing time, I told Osbert we had to leave.

He waddled over to me, but I knew he felt at home in the Penguin Palace. It had everything he needed.

Osbert was the first Christmas present Santa ever gave me that I really wanted. I had asked for Osbert, and I had gotten him.

But Osbert needed ice slides and leopard seals and plenty of herring. I asked him if he would be happier living at the Penguin Palace. Osbert looked into my eyes. And then he nodded.

It's a little lonely at home without Osbert. And my new sweater itches my neck a little bit, right under my chin.

But it's nice to be warm. And I had chocolate chip waffles for breakfast!

Next Saturday is Kids Visit Free Day at Antarctic World. I don't have bus fare, but I can walk. I'll wear my red sweater so Osbert will be sure to recognize me.

And next Christmas is only eleven months away!

I've thought about it a lot, and I already know what I want.

I'm sure I can't get into too much trouble with just one helicopter.